STICK MAN

The Little Stickman

BERTHA VALENTINE

STICK MAN
Copyright © 2021 **Bertha Valentine**

Stratton Press Publishing
831 N Tatnall Street Suite M #188,
Wilmington, DE 19801
www.stratton-press.com
1-888-323-7009

ISBN (Paperback): 978-1-64895-625-6
ISBN (Ebook): 978-1-64895-626-3

Printed in the United States of America

The kingdom was at peace at last after many years of war. King Givefree had finally won and his people could now reap the benefits of their bounty. "There will never be war here again." The king had given his word that for as long as he lived, neither he nor his decedents would ever allow another war.

The king had been ruthless in his battles, and his people had suffered for many had died in the war. The king himself had lost his wife. She was killed with their daughter wrapped in her arms. The king's servants fought the enemies to the last man, but in the end, the only one to survive in the palace was the little Princess Shyanna.

At that moment, the king's whole life changed as he looked around at the bodies of the people he had known all his life—people who had dressed him, cleaned for him, and kept his house in order. These people were not a part of his army; they were just caretakers, and they lost their lives in the care of his family. He would never let this happen to his family or his people again.

After that night, he fought with purpose for his daughter, his people; and with the help of his people, they won. But the war had left their land and treasury depleted, burning fields unsuited for planting, and no money to even buy seeds left the kingdom at the point of starvation.

There was no choice. The king decided to take an escort of soldiers to the next kingdom to request help. But to do that, they would have to travel through the place called the Dark Wood.

Every kingdom avoided the Dark Wood, a place that even birds did not fly over. It was said no sun could penetrate the trees of the wood, and as far as anyone in the kingdom knew, no one lived or had ever lived in the wood. They arrived at the Dark Wood just before dark. The sergeant of the guard suggested they go around the woods.

"It would be a least a week longer, and our people cannot wait that long. We must forge ahead into the woods," said the king.

"But, Your Majesty, your daughter?" the soldier questioned.

The king had brought his baby girl, for she had not left his side since her mother's death. He had declared they would die or live together. This was no different; he could not protect her if she was not with him.

"She will be fine because we are together, but let us wait until the morning to traverse the Dark Wood."

The soldier seemed content with that, and soon everyone had bedded down for the night. But the king who was having trouble with his baby daughter sleeping could not rest. He sang to her, he walked with her, he played with her, yet she would not sleep. He took out a little milk because they did not have a lot to spare. He fed her a little. She was so thin as he watched her suck down the almost empty bottle. Looking up into the starry sky, he whispered, "Please help me to help my people. For if they grow, we grow. And, Lord, I need my daughter to grow."

In the darkness, someone watched, and his heart went out to the unfortunate king as he watched him divide the small amount of milk, a little now and a little later for his baby, yet still not enough. The baby still cried through the night from hunger as a result. The party slept later than they should have. It was midday before anyone woke.

"This place!" the king declared as he jumped to his feet from his bedroll.

"Your Majesty!" his sergeant at arms rushed in.

"I know. We are late," the king grumbled as he glanced at his small baby.

"No, that is not…Please come see this, Majesty!" The soldier was so excited.

The baby started to cry once more, stopping the ling in his tracks. "Please, Your Majesty, this is important."

The king raised his daughter in his arms and followed his man outside his tent. There in the middle of their camp was a wooden table set up while they were asleep, and on the table was food and drink for the men and milk for little Shyanna.

The whole group was astonished for never had they seen such a bountiful feast—fruit and meat and wonderful sweet juice was all there to eat.

The king stood fast. "This must be a trick! We must not eat this! Men, gather your things. We must leave here!"

The men went about collecting their things, but the food stood before them like water in the wasteland. Even baby Shyanna had emptied the last of her milk and started to cry deeply. Her belly was still empty!

None of the men had eaten. The Dark Wood was their only opportunity to hunt, but now they had food set before them, why should they hunt?

One of the men just stood and stared at the table of food. "Sir, I will be the first to taste the food. If it is poison, allow me to be the sacrifice in the name of our land."

"No!" the sergeant yelled. "We are all hungry, but we most stand our ground."

"And starve." The king stood forth as he grabbed an apple and bit down. All the men gasped as the king chewed and swallowed the fruit. "It is good," he declared. "Sit. Let us give thanks to the spirits who have supplied these gifts."

They did and ate until full, taking the rest of the food to help feed them on their way. The Dark Wood was very dark as expected, but for some reason, they moved through it quickly as if the forest itself helped them by showing them the pathway through.

It was late afternoon when they arrived at the Kingdom of Were. The prince refused to see King Givefree or even listen to his pleas for his people.

King Givefree did not let it stand. He moved his men to the outside of city of Were; however, the young king heard of their camp site and decided to pay them a visit. He demanded that the king leave his kingdom, "You have won your battles. Why, pray, are you here? Certainly not to ask for help from us, the people you have defeated!"

"I have come to ask for help because when we defeated your father, we allowed you to keep your riches and land. We wanted nothing from you and for that reason your father, your king, said he was in my debt."

"So you seek to collect! We owe you nothing but your life, and when my father comes back from his business, he will be glad that I have done this. Now go with your lives and remember we owe you no more! Get off our land." His soldiers surrounded them with swords drawn!

"I came here because your father believed he owes a debt, and we could help each other. Now believe this, you will not be bothered with us again!"

As King Givefree's men were collecting their things, the prince's army attacked, killing many of the king's men and wounding the king himself!

He was forced to take Shyanna and run, leaving his few men to fight off the onslaught. As they reached the Dark Wood, the king could hear his men being slaughtered behind him!

"Run, mighty king!" he heard the prince yelling after him.

King Givefree went into the Dark Wood, holding his daughter close. It was already night, and he could see nothing in front of him, but he could hear as the prince and his army following them into the dark.

"You have no chance!" the prince yelled through the darkness.

"Why are you doing this? What can you gain from killing us?" the king yelled back as he lowered himself from his horse while still carrying his daughter.

"Everything—to kill the man who destroyed our kingdom and then allowed us out of some sympathy for our devastated people, to keep our land and riches means nothing! You should die and all of your offspring should die!"

The king moved quickly, holding his daughter to his chest. He wrapped his cape around her twice and tied it across his chest, anchoring her to him so his hands were free. He started to run, moving quickly; and with every step, he thought he saw small lights for his footing showing him where to step. Suddenly, a sound caught his ear, and he felt a sharp pain in his back. An arrow had hit him dead center in his back! He felt himself falling and rolled to his back, breaking the arrow as he did.

"Have we killed you yet?" the prince yelled out to the woods.

The king reached for the arrow but could not grab it. He took a deep breath and touched his baby on her head. Suddenly, something touched him, and he could feel the arrow slowly being removed from his back.

But how could this be? His back was on the ground. As he considered the arrow, pain burned the wound and he felt it ease, as if it was gone, and he knew the wound was gone.

"Stay and rest," he heard a soft whisper that only he could hear. "You have been a good king, father, and leader to your people. Because of this, we have decided to show you favor and give you all that your people need. We ask only that you do not allow anyone to ever harm the woods in any way shape or form."

Givefree felt blessed that something in the woods had saved them, so he agreed to keep the woods safe. A glowing light melted away any concerns he had, and he drifted off into a long deep slumber. Then the spirits turned their attention to the prince and his army men.

"Bringing war to the Dark Wood leaves you venerable to all that the woods can do," the words spread over them like a blanket, and when morning came, they were gone.

The next morning found the king and his daughter safe at the gates of their kingdom surrounded by a large pale of gold and another filled with jewels fine and rare.

King Givefree used this treasure to help his people and rebuild his land. He had food brought in from other lands, giving their own lands time to become fruitful again. Soon, the land became productive again, and his people started to grow their own food. He gave each house a piece of land, and each grew different crops. Soon, at harvesting time, a great celebration was held at the palace, which was rebuilt, and every family brought their crops. The king was filled with joy to see how far they had come, and on this occasion, he threw out to the people silver coins as a way of thanking them for their loyalty.

From that moment on, every harvest was celebrated in just that way with the king, giving silver or gold coins. The farmers supplied the palace, and because there was peace, the king put the army to work making paths to make it easy for the farmers to come and go to the palace and each other. Soon, the kingdom of Givefree thrived in food and land. But the King never forgot what happened in the Dark Wood. He built his kingdom closer to it, and soon made an agreement with the other kingdoms to buy the land. Each kingdom agreed, even the king of Were, who still searched for his son.

King Givefree went with his daughter to the Dark Wood every year on the day of the incident. He built a huge wooden table that would remain there, and every year, he placed a meal suited for a king dressed and ready for anyone who cared to eat there.

"Why do we do this every year, Daddy?" his daughter, who was now becoming a little girl, asked.

"We owe a debt, and I can never do enough to repay it."

They dressed the table, and the king placed Shyanna on her little pony. Her little dress was embedded with gold thread, and her shoes were made of glass with jewels embedded on the sides of her feet.

She was treated as a princess. Her father spared her nothing; anything she wanted, her father allowed, for he felt he could never fill her mother's shoes, therefore he must afford her nothing.

This idea would come back to curse him and his people for Shyanna would indeed grow.

The years passed, and she grew into a beautiful woman—brown-skinned, the color of brown sugar, just like her mother; her hair in waves of black floating behind her as she ran through the halls of the palace in pursuit of something she wished her father to get for her.

Over the years, she had become a black stain to the kingdom. Her attitude towards the people of the kingdom and their—as she declared it—taking her inheritance as her father gives it to them were sucking the kingdom dry and in doing so denying her the future she so richly deserves.

Shyanna spent most of her time browbeating the servants for such small occurrences as not making her bed the way she expected or sweeping dust too close to her shoe collection, not hanging her dresses as she wanted, and when she was not assaulting the palace servants, she was making the whole of the kingdom bow to her. She was running her horse and carriage through the crop fields whenever she desired, ruining many for the farmers. Her father, the king, paid to replace them and everything else she managed to destroy.

"Father, we are royalty. They should be honored that I have paid any attention to them at all! I am a princess. I am supposed to be able to do whatever I want and, Father, you are too." She stamped her feet as she yelled at him.

The king was getting old, the wars he had fight so hard in was now taking their toll, his body ached from many years of fighting in campaigns. So many wars he had seen, and now to start another with his daughter, he couldn't. His heart could not take it!

Shyanna became a menace as she started to take over little bits of the kingdom without the king's permission. When asked by her father, she denied it until one of the old soldiers stood up, telling the truth of it.

"She has used the treasury money for her own gain, Your Majesty."

"What is she doing with the treasury money?"

"Father, if you must know, I am engaging an army to take over the kingdom. I wanted to wait until you died, but I changed my mind."

"What!" the king said in shock. "I cannot believe that you would do this!"

"Father, I do love you, but you are weak. I could rule this kingdom with an iron hand and make it what it once was."

"It was a kingdom of war and death. The way we were killed your mother and left you without her." He was angry at the thought that she would want the old ways for their people!

"Father, a lot of the younger people believe as I do. They want more than fields and work. They want the thrill of battle," Shyanna started to explain.

"You and your followers have no idea what you are saying. I will not allow you and your selfish ways to put this kingdom back in war." He motioned to the guards. "Take her to her chambers and take her cohorts to the edge of the Kingdom of Givefree and make sure they leave and never come back!"

All the older people gathered together pushing the so-called army of Shyanna out of the city with fits of rage, for they too had worked hard to overcome their past. Keeping the peace in their kingdom and upholding what they had built was important to everyone.

The king considered his daughter's control over the kingdom. She was his only child therefore his only blood-line to the throne. He could not just exile his only child. He must find a way for her to still be queen without any power.

After days of thought and consultation with his closest friends, he addressed the whole kingdom, "My daughter is to be married. We will arrange a party of all the kingdoms.

Each king will send his son to visit our kingdom and meet my daughter in the hopes one of them will find her pleasant for marriage."

Everyone in the kingdom clapped and cheered at the king's idea, for everyone wished the best for her.

Shyanna heard the speech also, and she would have none of it. "How dare Father decide my future! I will be a great queen and a wonderful ruler! Of course, the servants would have to obey. They will have to do that anyway. Married or not, I am still their queen, and I will make them yield to my wishes!"

"You will not have a choice." Givefree had come into her chambers from outside after overhearing her remarks. "My child, these people have helped us through some rough times. They could have left us after the war when we could not even feed ourselves, much less our own house servants, yet the soldiers and their families stayed. They swore to keep you safe and they did indeed. We owe them our gratitude and our loyalty. We must appreciate what they have risked for this kingdom."

"Father, we must appreciate nothing! We are their rulers, and they will bow to us or fall! We own them and their land and what they make from that land! You allow them to keep the crops, I say I will keep the product and give them what I want them to have! You make them more than what they really are. Servants are just made to serve, and I will give them a real ruler to serve, and they will be glade of it!" Her beautiful face was dark with arrogance. All her life she had watched as her father treated the servants as equals. He had brought them houses and gave them land, even going so far as to break the ground to make passes so they could make their way to the palace, so they could leech more money from him.

She hated her father because he was weak! He cared about them, his people, and for what? What had they done for him, more importantly what had they done for their new queen, and what won't they do when she ruled with power?

The king watched the look on his daughter's face, and he knew he had made the right choice. "You will be married, and then you will leave this kingdom and go to your own. This kingdom will never be yours." The king turned and left her in her chambers alone.

Shyanna screamed with the horror of her soul, realizing that she would never be the queen she wanted to become thanks to her father, the king! She had to do something, but what? She had already tried a revolution; the only thing that accomplished was her men being exiled.

No, this time she had to try using what she knew of her father. She had to use his nature against him. His feelings for her had always been a weak point; he would never see her hurt in any way. So if she could pretend to be in some kind of life-threatening predicament, he would be so happy to have her back safe and sound that he would forget about her bad behavior.

15

To make sure they would not find her too readily, she decided to go to the Dark Wood, for only her father would go there, but only to stand outside it, he would never go into the woods, therefore he was afraid! She had been with him every year to his dinner to honor his lost men, not once did he ever go into the woods that she could remember.

Shyanna waited until dark then eased from her chambers and out of the palace, being always the best-dressed princess in the Dark Wood. She had brought a change of clothing for when she was found. In her mind, she had played out the scene. Her father would slice through the Dark Wood, dark trees hurling from the force of his blows! He would suddenly see her dressed in her moonlight jewel dress, the one that glowed in the darkness. When he spots her there crying and sitting in a field of the greenest grass her mind could conjure up, when he sees her there in her beauty, he will be transfixed to a time when she was his baby girl and nothing was good enough for her! He will be under her spell once more.

But her plan quickly went down for as she started to make her way to the Dark Wood, rain poured down, and her shoes made of gold did not traverse over the dirt and rocky roads easily.

Soon they were stuck in the mud, and she traveled through the night barefooted. Her beautiful hair was drenched along with the rest of her, but soon she was at the Dark Wood. As she arrived, she took a deep breath and lifted her dress to step over a log and suddenly felt herself falling. When she looked up at the darkness around her, she knew she was on the ground covered in mud and marsh.

She broke the silence of the night with a shriek that hurt the ears of any living thing within hearing distance. "I hate outside. The nasty, filthy, disgusting nature of it all messing up my dress! Father had better come soon, and when he does, I will become queen and destroy this awful place!"

Shyanna never really liked being outside. She was always an inside child and since her father had been attacked by the prince of Were, he did everything to protect her even if it meant not acquainting her with the world. He thought to only protect her, yet now she was someone the king did not recognize. Even she had considered that she did not belong for her father loved being out among his land and people; he took great joy in being out in the fields working with his hands and people. She could remember watching him laughing and smiling and working hard beside his servants. *Crazy!* she thought as she remembered.

She stood trying to wipe the mud from her dress. "Nature has no respect for how long it takes for me to look good."

It was late as she made her way into the interior of the woods; it was so dark that she could not see her footing. She looked back as the light of her old life disappeared and smiled for she reasoned that when she emerged from this darkness and into her new life, the queen of her Kingdom.

It felt to her like she was moving into a hole. With every step, the darkness covered her until she could see no light. Her feet were wet and mud-soaked and to her it felt as if she was walking through thick cold sand. She had fallen so many times that she could not feel which way was up. Soon the darkness had gotten to her, and she started to cry. "I hate this place. This place is horror, and when I get home, it is gone!"

The Dark Wood was precisely the name for it was darker than dark, and Shyanna soon felt lost.

Morning had come, but it was still dark to her for in the wood there was no sun ever. The trees seemed to come together to keep the sun from breaking through. Days passed and Shyanna was tired and hungry, her hair dirty with leaves and dried mud stuck in it. Her dress was covered in filth, her feet and hands covered in earth. She cried constantly for she had always been cared for; this was unheard of for her. "Why has Father not come for me? He always comes for me! FATHER!" she yelled. "I am a princess. They cannot just forget about me! I am their queen, the reason for their being." She laughed out loud suddenly. "They will come for me, and when they do, I will have them beaten within inches of their lives for making me wait so long." She laughed again—an evil, hideous laugh that came from her soul.

"Be still!" a voice came from the darkness to touch her ear.

Shyanna was shocked into silence, but then bounced back quickly to yell, "Here, I knew you would come! I am your princess and I am dirty and my dress is filthy and I think I am standing in something I know not what, so I command you to come here now and get me!"

"Rest your mouth. You have been talking nonstop since you walked into this place!"

"Who said that?" She started to run.

"Where are you going? You cannot see where you are going."

Shyanna did not care. She ran through the muck, getting her foot stuck in the heavy mud. As she moved, it went up her thigh, and she screamed as she felt it!

"OOOHHHHH…How I hate this place." Anger reared up from her as she fought to release herself! "I want to go home. They should have found me by now. They are inept! Father, you and your soldiers are unfit to find me just as you are unfit to run the kingdom." She broke out in tears.

"Here." She felt her body being raised from the mud.

"Who is there?" she asked, trying to see in front of her.

"I am Stick Man," he announced as he placed her on what seemed to be solid ground for the first time.

"Where are you?" She was trying to see anything. "You must listen. I need to go home, and if you help me, I will give you your heart's desire."

"My heart does not need much," the voice softly touched her ears.

"Then how about I do not burn your woods to the ground when I get out of here and trust and believe I will get out, and when I do, the first thing that I will do is to order my servants to burn it!"

"Huh, huh, huh" was all she heard.

"How dare you laugh at me! I am a princess and one day queen of the land surrounding this place. You will obey my wishes as a servant of the realm!"

"Mmmmm..." was all she heard.

"Hello...Hello, are you there?" she asked, trying to see anything.

He was gone, and no matter how much screaming and yelling she did for him to come, he did not. Another day passed. Shyanna was crying and sitting where he had left her. She was hungry and thirsty. Suddenly, something dropped in her lap, a bottle of water and a small pouch of food."

"There is food for you to eat. You must eat or die."

"I want to go home!" she announced stubbornly.

"I cannot take you home. I have never left the woods, and I cannot now."

Shyanna stood looking up at where she thought the voice was coming. "I will give you anything. Just help me home and whatever you wish is yours."

"Anything I wish?"

"Name it, and it is yours!" she pleaded.

"Your hand in marriage is all I want. If you give me that, then I will help you home."

"I am not going to marry someone I have never even seen! How do I know you have not planned this?"

"The plan was yours. Now do you accept my offer?"

"No, never. I am your princess, and I will not be extorted into marriage by some know-nothing savage living in the trees!"

"Your choice." He was gone, leaving her there in the dark with warm water and bread.

An hour later as he sat in the trees over her head, she said, "Okay, did you hear me?" She was frustrated and tried. "I will marry you. I want to go home now!"

"By all means, I will come for you in three days, and we will be married by your father, the king."

"Alright, alright...I want to go home now!"

"Be ready in three days."

"Fine. Now come down here and show me the way home." But before the words left her tongue, she was already back in her chambers. She looked around in disbelief. He had kept his word, and she was home! Her heart sang with joy, and she danced around her room! Home never felt so wonderful! "I will never leave it again!" She ran out to look for her father, and when she found him, he was on his throne worried that they would never find her.

When he heard her voice, his face lit up, and the dark clouds of worry left him! He ran to her, raising her into the air like she was his little girl again! She had not seen him so happy to see her in years.

"Look at you." He looked down at her dress. "You are filthy. Go and get clean. Maidens, help her please."

"Please…That is why I left here to make you think. They are our lesser, and we should not have to ask them or beg them to help us! We are superior to them in every way! Now come, peasants, and help me clean myself."

The king's heart sank once more. Shyanna would never learn, and he understood now that he could never leave her as queen. His head bent, and he started to weep at his only child. How could she be so? He had raised her to love and care for her people, but for some reason, she had lost her humanity for her own people, and now saw them only as chattels.

He and his people were one unit; whatever he felt, they felt for they were one. He worked right beside them, and they saw him as one of them.

He worried into the night, listening to Shyanna yell at her servants and throw glasses and chairs at them because she felt they did not move fast enough under her orders. "You will be the first one I throw in the dungeons when I become queen!"

Toward morning, the king sent for his messengers. He needed to arrange for his daughter's hand to—at this point—anyone!

As the messengers walked in, a light bright as the sun washed though the king's court. A green vine eased from the stone in the floor in the middle of the light. As the vine grew, it spread, making a ball of green. It grew larger and larger until it was huge then suddenly it spread and opened, and a creature resembling a log with sticks for arms and legs and fern leaves for hair stepped from it.

The king gasped in shock for he had never seen anything like the Stick Man. "Who are you?" the king asked, trying to stay calm, for he represented his kingdom.

"I am what you see, the Stick Man. I live in the Dark Wood, and I am here to arrange my wedding with my intended." The Stick Man walked around the room as he spoke, for it had been years since he had seen the inside of any house or palace.

His twig fingers were long and thin, and when he reached out for a vase that was placed on a table just beside the chamber door, the king marveled at the way his wooden fingers moved. He was magic from the woods, the very same woods that had saved him and his daughter's life years ago.

"What do you mean intended? Who is your intended?" The king watched him, entranced at his being.

The Stick Man looked back at him squarely. "Your daughter had consented to give me her hand in marriage."

"My daughter?"

"Yes. We are to be married in this kingdom in three days."

"How can that be? I do not understand." The king looked at him straight.

"Shyanna came to my home, the woods, and was lost. She begged me to take her home. She offered anything, and I asked her for her hand and she agreed." His answer had the ring of truth; however, he would have to ask Shyanna. The king looked at the Stick Man once more, knowing her as he did, he knew Shyanna would keep silent about her deal. "Why did you come to me instead of Shyanna for it was she who made the deal?"

"When she agreed to the offer, I asked that the celebration be held here and you act as officiate in our wedding. In that matter"—he moved to the king as if he had a secret—"I come to you for I know she is your only child, and I would not be a good man even as I am a wooden one if I did not ask you as her father for her hand in marriage."

"You are asking for my permission?"

"Yes, for I am old-fashioned in these matters."

"I see." The king smiled at him for he found him to be honorable both in his manner and in his ways. "I must converse with my daughter in the morn, so I ask you, please come back in the noon day and you will have your answer."

"As you wish," the Stick Man said and disappeared into the vines from where he came.

The sun shone through Shyanna's chambers as she opened her eyes to the world in which she had known since she was a little girl. It had all been a dream—the darkness and mud and wet, everything she hated. Shyanna had made them burn the dresses, and now she could just forget about that dreadful episode of her dark life. She stretched out in her bed and felt the silken sheets under her sore bottom. Her maiden had scrubbed her body at her request, and when it started to hurt her delicate skin, Shyanna bit and kicked them ,throwing things as they ran for protection from her. She cursed them for their rough treatment, forgetting it was at her request, but that did not matter at all.

Shy lay in her bed for hours after the sun rose. Her maids brought her food and water. She yelled at them with every step they took. Her father listened to her insistent yelling until he could take no more!

Walking down the hall to her chambers, he found one maid in tears outside her door. He placed his hand on her shoulder and smiled. "Go, my child. Go rest." The maid lowered her head and stood moving down the hall in the other direction.

The king had grown tired of her constantly degrading of his people; there was a brief serenity in her absence that he, now with her presence, missed. He stood now at her door feeling as if he was facing a foe on the battlefield. He opened the door, and there she was his only child. Stepping in, he said nothing at first. "Father, I am so glad you are here to see how badly they treat me!"

"I see, and after all that you have been through in the Dark Wood."

"Yes, Father, it was horrible and dark and wet, and I was so sore when I came home and these brutes tried to scrub my skin off! Father, can I have them whipped?"

The king ignored her ravings. "How did you get back home?" he asked, being very frank.

"What do you mean?" she asked, trying to act shocked at his question.

"We could not find you. You, by your own admission, talk of nothing but darkness. So I ask, how did you get in the palace?"

"Father, I had help. A voice came to me and helped me back home. It said I was the real queen of this land, and it helped me."

"That was all it said? It did not wish anything in return for helping a princess home."

"No. He was very helpful and said he would come by in three days to collect a reward."

"So he did want something in return?"

"Yes, Father. He wanted my hand in marriage, but he will just have to be contented with a little gold piece!"

The king said nothing for a moment. "You will keep you word to him because a princess always keeps her word."

"But I do not even know what he looks like! He could look like a monster!"

"You should have considered that before you gave your consent," he said as he walked past her and out of her rooms.

At noon, the Stick Man appeared; and for the first time, Shyanna saw her fiancé and her reaction was less than contented. She screamed until she was hoarse, and she could not speak.

"She is excited at the sight of you," the king supplied as she screamed. "These are screams of joy!"

The Stick Man watched her through eyes as green as a summer day, and then looked at her father. "You do not have to console my spirit, for I know what I am and I know what she sees. I am content if she has agreed to the arrangement."

"But I do not agree," Shyanna protested hoarsely. "I cannot marry a thing like that!"

Her father suddenly turned on her, grabbing her by her elbow; then pardoning himself and his daughter, he escorted her from the room.

"You will do as you have promised for the word of the royal is law! You are my child, and as such, you are of royal blood. Yes?" He waited for her answer.

Shyanna had never denied her royal blood and her right to be the next ruler of her father's kingdom. Now that very fact was sealing her fate. If she said she would not marry the Stick Man, he could refute right to the throne. "Father, I only said I would marry him so I could come home! I cannot marry that thing. I am a princess of your throne, and I cannot share my throne with that creature!"

"You have given your word as a princess of this throne, and it was you who left here thinking to change my heart. Now you have, by approving to this being's agreement, yielded your right to my throne! You, my child, will marry him because it is our duty as royalty to stand by our word, for it is the law of our land. Now let me be the first to congratulate you on your nuptials." The king turned and walked back into his throne room with Shyanna being dragged by his hand.

"Please, please, Father, do not make me marry this... this..."

"You may call me Stick Man," the wooden creature supplied.

"You will be a welcome addition to our family, Stick Man, and I will be glad to marry you here in two days."

"Does Shyanna feel the same?"

The king looked back at his daughter now standing at the edge of the door. She looked up as all eyes turned to her. She could not relent and have all her people look at her as a weak princess; her word must be like iron to them. She would marry him, but she would be back to become their queen. With a look filled with cold tranquility, she bowed her head in a yes.

"Good. Now this is a time to celebrate. Stick Man, stay and enjoy the festivities of our kingdom before the wedding!"

"I cannot," Stick Man said as he watched his princess's face. She was still with rage, and he felt her anger for him, but soon she would change. "I must leave to arrange our new home, a place to bring my new bride."

"We are not living in the Dark Wood, are we?" Shyanna yelled in fear.

"No. I will show you the wonders of the woods, starting with our palace in the mountains. I will return in two days. Until then, enjoy your people." He moved to stand in front of Shyanna. Bending over, he kissed her hand then disappeared.

The whole of the kingdom danced in the streets for two days, even the king danced. Shyanna watched, and as she did, her anger grew into rage. She hated her people and the Stick Man, but more and more, she was starting to hate her father. How could he allow this? She had thought that he loved her. Now here he is dancing and his only child being married to a monster—more precisely, he is marrying her to a monster! This was crazy to her!

She wanted to run away, but her every move was under constant watch. She never had a moment alone, which made her scream even more!

The day of her wedding was a blur, and all she could remember was the Stick Man showing up at the podium. Shyanna's mind reeled with plans of revenge, with her father at the top of the list. Her plans to kill him and take his throne may be beyond her now, but she knew sooner or later she would be back to gain her rightful place.

As the vows were read, the Stick Man took her in his stick arms and held her with his long twig fingers. Vines moved through the crowd and up around the Stick Man and his new bride, making a ball. As the vines encircled them, it became smaller and smaller as the vines spirited them away and soon one leaf of green swirled in the air, slowly fading away.

Shyanna was floating, and she opened her eyes to see her wooden husband holding her close. Looking down, they were high in the air over her father's kingdom. "How can this be?" she asked, pulling him closer around his log neck.

"Magic at its purest. There is nothing like it."

She was in awe of her husband's power. "Can you teach me how to do this?" she asked, looking at him straight in his log face.

"I can teach you this and much more." He was filled with pride as he looked down at her with his beautiful green eyes, the only humanity he had left.

"Where are you taking me?" Her voice was emotionless.

"To the Dark Wood, our home. I have made a place for you." They looked down as they descended.

"I cannot see anything in that horrid place! I do not wish to go. Put me down. I will not go." She tried to fight against him!

"Be calm and see what you have always wanted."

But Shyanna was not listening. She started to pull away from him as his twig toes touched the ground. She fell in the mud, yelling at him as she rose. But then she saw something through the murky woods and it glistened.

"How did you do that?" She was stunned at the sight.

A huge castle stood before her, shining with its golden walls, beautiful jewels embedded in the gold, and Shyanna could see it clearly even as the darkness surrounded it.

He smiled at her expression. For the first time, he noted that she was speechless. They walked into the castle silently as Shyanna took it all in. "This is all mine?"

"Yes. I have no use for jewels or gold, but I knew you have a love for it. I noticed when you were lost in the woods."

He watched as she walked through the whole castle. It was furnished in wood with gold and silver lining and curtains made of gold and silver. Shyanna looked around, finding it to be up to her expectations. For now, she would be able to go back and take her kingdom from her father.

Instead of someday, it will be tomorrow; and by tomorrow night, her father would be dethroned, and she would rule with an iron glove. She had enough treasure to buy an army. She could rule all five kingdoms with this treasure. She laughed out loud and danced for her fortune was right in front of her! As she danced, the Stick Man came into her view once more, and she suddenly stopped dancing.

She could not rule with this thing beside her! She was going to be a ruler of all. Her kingdom was going to be larger than any has ever had before! This little stick could not be by her side, she could not allow that!

"You must be hungry," the Stick Man said as he looked at her suddenly sad face.

Shyanna watched as he walked past her to the dining room. As she followed him in, she sat at the diamond-made table before a large fireplace made into the wall. She looked up to see it had faces of men, some reminding her of people from her own kingdom. "Who are the faces?"

"They are the men who brought war here to the wood. The spirits here do not like war of any kind. To bring war here is to be trapped here forever," he explained as he bent to the fireplace to make the fire.

As he bent toward the fire, cooking her first meal as his wife, Shyanna suddenly smiled, for now she realized she did not have to be queen with a thing for a husband.

As he placed the food on the table before her, she smiled at her fortune. "I am cold. Can you build the fire up?"

"Of course." He turned to the fire, bending over it. This time, blowing it with a bellows.

Shyanna watched as the fire grew, and when it was at its highest, she lifted her foot and kicked him into the flames! The fire blew out into the room, causing her to take cover from the flames! When the flames died, she inspected the fireplace to make sure the Stick Man was all gone.

There was no sign of his stick body anywhere. Shyanna laughed at the thought. Now there would be no one to stand in her way. She would have everything her heart desired and more!

She danced through the house until she was too tired to dance any more. Soon she grew sleepy, and she went upstairs to lie on her beautiful golden bed and silken sheets made of gold thread. She fell asleep dreaming of how she was going to rule and her new life.

The next morning, she woke slowly from a heavy sleep. She rubbed her hair, not feeling her silky locks. She pulled some out and in her hand was a leaf. She ran to the diamond mirror. What looked back at her was the Stick Woman!

She screamed, breaking the mirror as she fought her own reflection! "How could this happen! I am a princess. I cannot be a monster! No, I am supposed to be queen. I am supposed to be rich!"

As she was raving in anguish, she suddenly heard someone coming up the stairs. She ran hiding under the golden bed. She watched as two bare feet moved across the floor easily. Stepping to the bed, they stopped and she watched as a hand lowered beside the feet. "I know how lonely it will become here in the dark. I cannot see you going through this as I did, alone, I know you think you had your reasons—"

Stick Woman moved from under the bed. "How dare you feel sorry for me! I am a princess, and I WILL RULE MY KINGDOM! THIS I SWEAR!" She started to cry.

No more the Stick Man, the young king of the faraway land of Groon smiled at her, a perfect smile beautiful white teeth, and green eyes the color of summer leaves, a face framed them brown and sweet. "I was like you and became the Stick Man long ago. My family and friends…no one could save me. I hated them and I hated myself. So I am not going to allow you to go through this alone. We are married, and I want to take you home."

"No, I will not go. I am hideous. I will stay in the Dark Wood." Her voice was softer.

"Then I will stay."

"No," she said even softer.

"Then I will visit, for I know these woods as I know my home."

That is what he did. He visited her every day, bringing her food and dresses from his very rich kingdom. He waited for her until the curse was done and passed on.

CPSIA information can be obtained
at www.ICGtesting.com
Printed in the USA
BVHW031401221121
622225BV00003B/166